WHAT'S YOUR DREAM?

ANDERSON'S

HEAT

Sports Illustrated Kids What's Your Dream books
are published by Stone Arch Books

A Capstone Imprint

1710 Roe Crest Drive
North Mankato, Minnesota 56003
www.mycapstone.com

Library of Congress Cataloging-in-Publication Data is available
on the Library of Congress website:

ISBN: 978-1-4965-3441-5 (library binding)
ISBN: 978-1-4965-3445-3 (paperback)
ISBN: 978-1-4965-3449-1 (eBook PDF)

Designer: Russell Griesmer

Editor: Nate LeBoutillier

Production Specialist: Kathy McColley

Photo Credits:
Design Elements: Shutterstock

Printed and bound in the USA.
009657F16

WHAT'S
YOUR
DREAM?

ANDERSON'S HEAT

BY DEREK TELLIER

STONE ARCH BOOKS
a capstone imprint

CHAPTER ONE

Anderson hustled onto the baseball field. He was the first player to arrive.

Coach sat in the dugout. "Anderson," he said, "you look ready to play ball."

"I am."

Coach read some paperwork. He held up a few sheets. "New umpires this year. I can't wait."

Anderson smiled. He took his bat, grabbed a ball, and went to the backstop. He tossed the ball up and hit it into the fence. He grabbed the ball, tossed it up again, and smacked it into the fence. Other players showed up. They lollygagged from the parking lot to the diamond.

Coach yelled, "This ain't the Bigs. We hustle here."

Players started hustling.

Others joined Anderson at the fence. Bats smacked balls. Balls hit the fence. An eleven-year-old everyone called Tater Tot started belching. Other guys started. Coach came over. "You want to play ball, or you want to belch?"

A huge belch.

Coach laughed. "Take a lap."

Players ran from one end of the outfield to the other. Anderson led the pack, but not without conflict. Some guys tried to outrun him. Tater Tot sprinted to the front. Another player, Charlie Price, the catcher on the team, took the lead, until Anderson sped up and reclaimed it. The pack charged through the outfield. Charlie took the lead, then Tater Tot, but in the end, Anderson won the race across the foul line.

"Good hustle," Coach said. "That's what it'll take."

Tater Tot, Charlie, and Anderson fist-bumped.

Coach said, "Let's go. Eleven-year-olds."

The eleven-year-olds pumped their fists. They said "Hustle!"

Coach said, "Let's go. Twelve-year-olds."

The twelve-year-olds pumped their fists. They said "Hustle!"

"That's what it'll take," Coach said. "From the parking lot to the dugout. From the dugout to the outfield. From home plate to first base. From third base to home plate."

Guys pounded their fists into their mitts.

"No one will out-hustle us."

Guys pounded their fists.

Coach said, "The Little League World Series, that's where we're going."

Fists pounded mitts.

"We're the league's all-stars," said Coach, "but as we go into tournament play, we aren't players from different teams. We're all one team."

Guys fist-bumped whoever was standing next to them.

"We'll take districts. We'll take sectionals. We'll take state. We'll take regionals." Coach paused. "We'll take the whole thing. We'll take the Little League World Series."

Mitts smacked.

"And you know what else?" Coach asked. "We're going to have fun."

Fists on leather.

"We're going to have fun hustling out there. We're going to have fun sliding. We're going to have fun diving. We're going to have fun wiping the dirt off our uniforms. We're going to have fun taping up our fingers and wrists and knees. We. Are. Going. To. Have. Fun."

Dudes laughed.

"What are you laughing at?"

Tater Tot said, "I'm having fun."

"Well, good," Coach said. "Get to your positions."

Anderson raced Tater to shortstop. Once the season started, one would pitch and the other would play shortstop. As the team took infield, there was no need for a pitcher, so they both raced to shortstop. They tied. Anderson cut off the throw from center, spun, and gunned the ball home. Tater Tot covered second and caught the throw from right on a one-hop. Anderson barehanded a slow roller and fired on the run. Tater fielded one in the gap. Anderson grabbed a chopper and turned two. Tater caught a toss, slid his foot over second, and threw to first. Anderson covered third on a bunt.

Tater belched as loud as he could.

Coach said, "Did some kind of walrus invade the diamond?" He hit a fly to shallow left-center and told Tater to catch it.

Tater ran out and got camped, sort of. He fell over backward as he made the play.

At the plate, Anderson smashed two line drives and on the third pitch, went yard. He hit a couple of deep pop flies and then went yard again. Then he bounced one over the fence. He followed with a line drive that hooked foul over the third base line and ended with a few smashes into the outfield gaps.

Charlie said, "Nice work, Anders." Anders was short for Anderson.

Coach added, "Nice focus, Anders."

Tater Tot stepped to the plate. He swung at the first pitch and missed. With mock anger, he tapped the bat against home plate.

Charlie chimed in, "That one's out of here. It's a grand slam!"

Coach fell down. He said, "The wind on that one knocked me down."

"I'm having fun," Tater said. "I'm taking this yard."

Tater swung at the next pitch and missed. Dudes laughed. Charlie said, "What are you doing now?"

"Now I'm having fun for Anders."

Dad drove Anderson home and said that Sofia's test results came back. They would all talk at home.

At home, Dad and Anderson got out of the car and went into the house. Mom was putting things away. She said, "I'll get Sofia."

They sat down at the table. Mom said, "Sofia, do you want to tell him?"

She nodded. "I have leukemia."

Anderson said, "They're sure?"

Sofia nodded. "They're sure."

Dad said, "Lots of kids Sofia's age get leukemia. It's a very beatable form of cancer."

The grown-ups relayed information. Sofia had a disease called acute lymphoblastic leukemia. Her white blood cells had grown cancerous. They had multiplied when they shouldn't have and had caused Sofia to have nosebleeds and headaches.

About a month ago, Sofia had fallen down when she was walking through the living room. The doctors now suspected leukemia was to blame. One of the symptoms is loss of balance.

Anderson sat there and let his parents bombard him with words he hated: anemia, chemo, leukocytes, and radiation. Sofia hadn't been feeling well, but cancer? Anderson didn't know what to do. He didn't know what to say. He just felt squeezed.

Mom said, "We're going to fight this."

Dad said, "With everything we have."

Anderson tried to be strong, but the new words . . . *Anemia. Chemo. Leukocytes. Radiation.* They were like intruders. He wanted them to leave. Mom hugged him. Anderson wiped some tears from his cheeks. He looked around.

Mom and Dad cried, but Sofia remained calm. She said, "Mom's making enchiladas."

Dad got up and defrosted some hamburger in the microwave. He pre-heated the oven. Mom, Anderson, and Sofia chopped peppers, shredded cheese, and cut tomatoes. Sofia said, "Dad, why aren't you helping?"

"I'm heating the oven."

"Go and get the Uno cards," Sofia said. "You're going down."

Dad got the Uno cards. He dealt to the kids as Mom finished the enchiladas. Sofia took no prisoners. She played wild cards. She reversed the order. If Dad or Anderson played a card that made her lose her turn, the next time, she would make them draw four. She laid the same numbers and changed the colors. When Dad and Anderson finally got tired of getting beat, Sofia said, "Bam, what."

CHAPTER TWO

Coach said, "Let's go. Eleven-year-olds."

The eleven-year-olds pumped their fists. They said "Hustle!"

Coach said, "Let's go. Twelve-year-olds."

The twelve-year-olds pumped their fists. They said "Hustle!"

"Pitchers and catchers, to the bullpen. Infielders, outfielders, guess where you're going?"

Infielders and outfielders guessed they were going to the infield and outfield.

Anderson toed the dirt around the pitching rubber with his cleat. He was supposed to lean back and fire.

Charlie crouched behind the plate.

For now, Anderson didn't need to screw around with any breaking pitches. He had been ordered to pop the catcher's mitt as hard as he could.

He wound up.

The pitch . . . In the dirt.

Anderson caught Charlie's throw back to the mound, kicked some dirt away from the rubber, and wound up. The pitch was low. Anderson missed the strike zone again with his next two — four balls in four throws.

Tater Tot called him Wild Thing, and Coach smiled.

Anderson kept firing. He threw one strike in his next five pitches. He took off his hat and ran his fingers through his hair.

Coach said, "Grab a ball and throw it as hard as you can into the fence."

Anderson unloaded.

"Now," Coach said, "do it again."

The fence rattled. Anderson toed the rubber, wound up, and fired a strike. His next pitch was high, but the pop of Charlie's catcher's mitt aroused some chatter. *Way to fire, Anders. Way to fire, dude.*

He leaned back and threw a rocket right down the middle.

Again, the pitch popped Charlie's catcher's mitt. He was told to keep it up. Anderson threw the next pitch over Charlie's head and clanged it against the backstop. His next pitch was inside, so far inside that Charlie couldn't even reach it. The ball caromed to the backstop.

"Would it kill you to throw strikes?" Tater said. "Let's go, Anders."

Anderson didn't care for Tater's tone. Anderson reared back and threw. Charlie snagged the pitch about an inch outside the strike zone, but the velocity was impressive.

"All right, Anderson," Coach said. "That's good."

Infield grounders were next.

Anderson hustled to the line of infielders. Guys waited their turn to field a ground ball. As Anderson got settled, he looked back at the bullpen. Tater Tot popped Charlie's catcher's mitt with a hard strike right down the middle. It wouldn't kill Tater to throw strikes.

Anderson stepped up to field a grounder. It bounced up and knocked Anderson's cap off his head. He had to chase after the ball. Once he retrieved it, he fired it back in. He overthrew the dude shagging balls, who looked at him with some stink-eye.

The next time around, Anderson had to dive for a hard grounder in the gap. He fielded the ball, but when he got up to throw, it fell out of his glove. He picked up the ball and gunned it. The dude shagging caught it without any problem, but he kept on giving Anderson the stink-eye anyway.

Sofia suggested she and Anderson go to the ballfield after supper. Mom and Dad granted permission. The kids grabbed a batting helmet, a bat, and a bucket of balls. They tossed their mitts in the bucket, stuffed batting gloves in their pockets, and left. They walked down the sidewalk. Sofia said, "You going to make the World Series?"

"I thought so," Anderson said.

"Well, won't you?" asked Sofia.

Anderson said, "I don't know."

Sofia told him to stop being a downer.

"Aren't you scared?" asked Anderson.

"I'm scared of missing softball," she said.

They got to the park. Anderson unlocked the electrical box and flipped on the light switch — Mom and Dad had convinced the Park Council Chair to give them a key. Anderson lugged the bucket of balls out to the pitcher's mound. He tossed a few to Sofia. He said, "You afraid of losing your hair?"

She said, "I can wear a cap."

"Yeah, but the other stuff?" said Anderson.

Sofia said she was not scared.

"Would it kill you to be scared?" said Anderson.

"Would it kill me?" asked Sofia.

Anderson said, "Tater said that."

"Who?"

"Matt," said Anderson.

"You call Matt 'Tater'?"

"Yeah," said Anderson. "Don't ask."

The kids backed up and threw some long ones.

Anderson said, "Is your team going to the
World Series?"

"Not without me."

Sofia said they should play a game. She would hit
first. Anderson had to strike her out three times before
he could hit. Whoever had the most hits after three
innings would win. Pretty simple idea.

Sofia put on the helmet and readied the bat.

Anderson looked in.

Sofia tamped the dirt around home plate.

Anderson wound up and delivered.

Sofia hit a sharp ground ball to the right side between first and second.

Anderson wound up. He fired as hard as he could.

Sofia fouled the pitch back. *Strike one.*

Anderson dug a ball out of the bucket. The pitch . . .

Sofia slapped a shot up the middle and knocked over the bucket of balls. Baseballs rolled all over the diamond. Anderson put his hands on his hips. Sofia laughed. The kids rounded up the balls.

Anderson gunned a heater right over the plate.

Sofia fouled it back. *Strike one.*

Anderson threw a tricky off-speed breaking pitch that Sofia swung at and missed. *Strike two.*

He had two strikes on her and wanted to get an out. He was going to keep throwing breaking pitches.

Anderson delivered, but Sofia fouled it off.

Tater popped into Anderson's head and made him mad. Anderson imagined Tater Tot was at the plate. He fired . . . *Strike three!*

Sofia had two hits, and Anderson had one out in the top of the first. Sofia tapped the bat on home plate and got ready.

Anderson fired the ball, but Sofia did not swing. "Hold on," she said. She stepped out of the batter's box and wiped her nose. Blood was on her fingers. She wiped again and covered her entire hand in blood.

"You all right?" Anderson walked up. The blood spooked him.

"I'm all right."

"I'll call Mom."

Sofia held her sleeve to her nose. Anderson could hardly even dial.

CHAPTER THREE

The next few weeks were a series of nosebleeds, at least to Anderson. Nosebleeds and headaches. Sofia was the one enduring the pain, but for reasons Anderson couldn't understand, he was the one who spent a lot of time with his head buried in his pillow.

He raced his teammates across the outfield. He dove for balls hit between short-stop and third base. He wound up on the mound and fired. He fired and fired and fired.

In post-season tournament play, to advance to the Little League World Series, the team needed to win the district tournament, sectional tournament, state tournament, and regional tournament. For game one of the district tournament, Coach put Anderson on the mound.

Anderson fell behind the first batter 2-0.

Tater Tot started chattering. *Let's throw strikes, Anders. Throw strikes, good buddy. Let's throw strikes now.*

Anderson wished he would just shut up.

Charlie looked over at Coach. He got the sign. Breaking ball. The batter popped a foul that was caught by the third baseman. Coach said to stick with the breaking ball. Batter number two dribbled one to second and was thrown out. The batter hitting in the three-hole Anderson K'd in three pitches.

Charlie tossed the ball to the mound. The defense ran back, and the guys pounded their fists into their mitts. *Hustle!*

They hustled around the base paths. The lead-off man beat out a grounder hit deep in the hole. The next batter walked but ran as fast as he could down to first.

Tater Tot came up next. In a big exaggerated motion, he tamped the dirt around home plate. He lined the first pitch to left-center, and the ball bounced over the fence. The ball was out of play, and the runners still hustled — that was what it was going to take. Coach came out of the dugout and said so.

Anderson hit in the clean-up spot. He stepped to the plate with runners on second and third.

He didn't swing at the first pitch, a called strike on the outside corner.

The next pitch came in high. One and one.

The next . . . Meatball down the middle.

Anderson turned on it and drove it to deep left. The base runners hustled in. Anderson rounded second and kicked in to a higher gear. He saw the throw coming and headed for the other side of the bag. The third baseman applied the tag, but Anderson's foot had already reached.

Coach clapped his hands. "Nice hustle, Anders! Wipe that dirt off your pants! Hustle!"

Before the inning fizzled into history, the men had put five runs on the board.

Anderson hustled out to the mound. He felt good throwing his warm-ups but walked the first batter. His focus lost intensity. He'd been able to block out the words he hated, but now they were back and had multiplied. A new intruder wrapped a tentacle around Anderson's thoughts. The word *port* was the new intruder. Sofia now had a port, a heart-shaped device attached to her chest. A small tube ran out of the port and disappeared into Sofia's skin. The port had to be there for the chemo treatments. The doctors administered the chemo drugs through the port. To Anderson, this port looked painful and intrusive, and now it consumed his thoughts. He took off his cap and wiped some sweat out of his hair. He knew how to beat these intruders — bear down and throw strikes.

Coach signaled. He wanted a breaking ball. Anderson did not. They agreed, finally, on a fastball.

Anderson fired. The pitch was high and inside. The hitter moved his head out of the way and gave Anderson a dirty look.

Tater Tot stood over at shortstop. *Let's throw some strikes, Anders. Throw strikes, good buddy. Let's throw strikes now.*

About the only thing worse than Tater's stupid chatter was the port.

Coach wanted a slider, down and away. Anderson delivered, but the ball did not slide. It stayed in the middle, and the batter smashed it over the center fielder's head. The center fielder hustled and kept the hit to a double, but a run scored. Anderson still had a 5-1 lead, but he looked frustrated.

Coach said, "Runs are gonna score, Anders. You'll be all right."

The port took over Anderson's thoughts.

Anderson wanted to fire. It was time to get mad. It was time to battle. He was going to throw a heater down the pipe and challenge the batter, head on.

The pitch . . . Swing and a miss. *Strike one.*

Anderson wanted to keep throwing heat. No changeups. No curveballs. No junk. It was time to battle. He fired, and again, the batter swung and missed. *Strike two.*

Anderson led in the count 0-2. No way in the world was he throwing anything but a fastball. He delivered. The batter swung and missed. *Strike three!*

Next batter, Anderson wanted another fastball. His fastball was powerful. It could fight off the intruders. Anderson wound up. The pitch was a rocket but missed outside.

A thought of Sofia hit him like a line drive to the nose. After a chemo treatment, she had lain in a deep sleep, perfectly still with the covers pulled up to her chin. Sofia never slept like that. She usually mumbled and kicked and rearranged herself into crazy positions.

The stillness had spooked Anderson, and now the uneasy feeling had returned. A fastball could keep it at bay, maybe.

Coach wanted a curveball.

Anderson did not and held out for a heater. He fired. Again, the pitch was a rocket but missed the strike zone down and away.

Charlie stood up. He said, "Anders, calm down. You're trying too hard."

Anderson realized he would have to throw a breaking pitch. He went ahead and nodded.

The off-speed pitch came in . . . The batter was out in front and drove the ball foul.

Anderson moved to 2-1, but the foul was hit so hard it made Anderson nervous. He felt like everything was suddenly against him.

And then Tater started in with his stupid chatter.

Let's throw strikes, Anders. Throw strikes, good buddy. Let's throw strikes now.

Coach wanted a curve.

Anderson was tired of disagreeing. He nodded, wound up, and threw. The curve did not curve. The ball hit the batter in the shoulder.

Anderson got pulled later in the inning. They won districts, but he couldn't sleep that night. He felt disappointed he hadn't played up to his potential.

He would need to play better at sectionals, or the team would never make it out alive.

CHAPTER FOUR

Anderson walked the hallway of his house. He was shoving pita chips into his mouth as fast as he could. He walked by Sofia's room. Her door was open. She sat up in bed, looking at her notebook computer. Anderson went in. "Playing *Minecraft*?" he asked.

Sofia said, "I'm playing *Ogre's Ice Cream*."

Anderson said, "*Ogre's Ice Cream*?"

"If I play *Minecraft* one more time . . . "

Anderson sat down on Sofia's bed. He tried to settle in so he could see but didn't want to jostle the pillows. Sofia sat all propped up. She didn't have any hair. She didn't wear a hat. She didn't care.

Anderson could see the outline of her port under her T-shirt. He offered some chips, but she didn't want any. She played a game in which an Ogre had to eat an ice cream cone before it melted. She lost. Sofia and Anderson laughed. The ogre was covered in ice cream. It was pretty stupid, but they laughed anyway.

Mom came in. "Sofia, how do enchiladas sound?"

"Awesome."

Mom asked if the kids wanted to help.

Anderson got up. He started toward the kitchen. He thought Sofia would be right behind him. He had to stop and look. She struggled to get out of bed. Mom helped.

Anderson went back, offered his arm. Sofia's bare head brushed against his cheek. The smoothness caught Anderson off guard. He let his arm slack. Sofia slipped, but Anderson and Mom recovered. They held her up.

Sofia said, "I'm gonna kill you in Uno."

They walked to the kitchen. Mom grabbed some peppers. Anderson got the knives. Sofia opened the cupboard and pulled out a cutting board — the slowness of her movements worried Anderson. They cut some peppers and moved on to onions. Anderson looked over and saw tears on Sofia's face. He didn't know if they were from the onions or something else.

Sofia sat down. She didn't want to play Uno. She didn't want any enchiladas.

In the finals of sectionals, Anderson battled on the mound. It was the top of the sixth, the final inning, with the score tied. Anderson had allowed runners on first and second.

Charlie came out from behind the plate. He put his hand on Anderson's shoulder. "Anders," he said. "Let's step off and get settled."

Anderson walked off the mound.

He took off his hat and wiped sweat out of his hair. It wasn't bothering him — it was just what he did when he pitched. Charlie kept his hand on Anderson's shoulder. They walked around for a moment. Charlie patted him on the back and hustled back behind the plate.

Coach called for a breaking pitch. Anderson shook him off, but Coach insisted.

Charlie got settled, low and inside. Anderson wanted to throw a fastball. He felt the most confident with a fastball, and the game was in the final inning.

Anderson leaned back and threw a fastball, right down the middle. The batter swung and missed. Charlie readjusted and snagged the pitch.

Coach ran out. He motioned for Tater Tot to come pitch. "Anders," he said. "Let's go take a seat."

Anderson took a seat. Coach sat down beside him but said nothing. Anderson realized he should have thrown a breaking ball as Coach had requested.

Tater Tot got through the inning without any damage. Guys hustled back to the dugout. Batters put on helmets and grabbed bats. They loaded them up with weights and took practice cuts.

"Here comes the bottom of the order," said Coach. "Seven, eight, nine, then the top. Let's go!"

Charlie led off by belting a single to left. The next hitter moved him over to second with a single to right. The guy in the nine-spot hit a slow roller to the second baseman but advanced the runners. Then, the lead-off hitter struck out.

Runners on second and third. Two down in the bottom of the sixth.

The two-hitter came to the plate. He took ball one high. Next pitch . . . foul, right off his shin. The hitter went down. Coaches ran out.

The batter got up, kind of. He was gimpy. The coaches looked at each other and discussed something Anderson could not hear.

Coach ran back to the dugout. He said, "Anders, you got your head out of your butt?"

Anderson had to think. He got up, put on his batting gloves, and secured his bat. He then walked up to the plate to pinch hit.

The pitch . . . Anderson swung and missed.

The next? A swing and a miss.

Anderson stepped out.

Third Base Coach went through signals. None of them were important.

Anderson knew he had to swing away. He took a practice cut. He saw his mom and dad in the bleachers. They were helping Sofia walk down the steps.

Anderson dug in his cleat, tapped his bat on the plate, and prepared.

CLINK! Aluminum hit cowhide.

The ball flew into left field. Charlie scored from third base.

Anderson hustled down the first base line. He tapped his foot on the bag to make the hit official. First Base Coach gave Anderson a big high-five.

They had just won the sectional tournament and taken another step toward the Little League World Series, but Anderson did not feel worthy of congratulations. He hadn't played his best ball and had disobeyed his coach.

To make matters worse, Anderson noticed that Sofia had fallen down and that Mom and Dad were trying to help her up.

CHAPTER FIVE

Anderson put together a puzzle as he watched a ballgame on television. All kinds of giggling came from Sofia's room. Friends from her softball team had come to visit. One of them had seen a new comedy movie and was revealing the plot, stupid joke after stupid joke. Every thirty seconds, laughter echoed down the hall.

Anderson turned up the television.

The girls giggled. One said, "Anders, come on. Turn up the volume."

"It won't go any higher," he said.

"Put it through the sub-woofer," said one girl.

Anderson said, "We don't have a sub-woofer."

One girl said, "Put it through a megaphone."

Anderson told them to shut up. He turned the television down a bit. His team was getting killed, and paying attention was not fun. There was a picture of a spaceship on his puzzle. Taking off on a spaceship and not coming back seemed like a good idea. Ten, nine, eight, seven . . .

The girls calmed down. One of them said, "We have a surprise."

For a while, Anderson heard only the play-by-play announcing of the baseball game, but then he thought he heard sniffling. He walked down the hall. He didn't want them knowing he was spying on them, so he made an effort to be quiet.

The girls were indeed crying. Somehow, they knew he was standing by the door and told him to come in.

Sofia held up a blue ribbon. She showed it to Anderson. "Know what this is?" she said.

"I think so."

One of the friends said, "We're sewing these ribbons on our uniforms. To honor Sofia."

"Cool," said Anderson. He looked around. Tears rolled off the girls' cheeks. He felt a lump forming in his throat and didn't want them to see him crying. He walked out.

Anderson decided to go outside and take a few rips. He hauled a bat and bucket of balls to the fence. He tossed the ball up and hit it into the fence. He grabbed another ball, tossed it up, and smacked it into the fence. He felt the lump in his throat returning.

His bat smacked the balls. Balls hit the fence. The process kept the tears at bay, until . . .

He wiped a tear off his face and went in the garage. He kneeled down and buried his face in the crook of his elbow. The sobs shook his entire body. He heard the door open, so he ran out of the garage and went around the corner of the house. He put his head against the siding. He couldn't believe what was happening. He had seen teams sew ribbons on their uniforms, but it was the kind of thing done by other people. Now that it was happening to Sofia, Anderson wanted to crawl in a hole. He felt small and afraid, and he wasn't even the one with leukemia. He figured Sofia was about a million times stronger than he was. He hated the entire situation.

All the new words, intruders that they were, dive bombed him like a swarm of hornets. *Anemia. Chemo. Leukocytes. Radiation. Port.*

He decided to go for a bike ride. He told Mom and hit the road. Anderson stood as he pedaled. His destination was not clear, but he wanted to get there as quickly as possible.

The muscles in his legs pushed the money in his pocket into an outline on his pants. Dad had told him once, "It ain't a bad idea to have a few bucks on you. You might need to stop somewhere and buy a hotdog. You never know."

After being given such advice, Anderson started carrying a few bucks.

He heard an announcer's voice echo out of a public address system. *Batting fifth is . . .* He heard cheers. A ballgame was going on, so he rode toward it.

As he neared the park, Anderson thought he might swing by the concession stand. They sold great hotdogs, and he had a few bucks in his pocket.

Why not?

No ketchup. No mustard. No relish. Only hotdog and bun. Sofia smothered her hotdogs in ketchup. Yuck. Talk about ruining a good hotdog. Anderson sat on his bike and chomped.

Girls about Sofia's age played a tightly contested game. It was 6-5 in the fifth. The batter hit a grounder to shortstop. The fielder bobbled the ball, and the runner beat out the throw. The runner over-ran first, and when she turned around, she turned to the left and trotted back in fair territory.

Mom and Dad had taught both Anderson and Sofia not to do such a thing. Mom and Dad had said to turn right and run back in foul territory. If the umpire thought you were rounding the bag and trying for second, an infielder could tag you out. It was best to leave no doubt in the umpire's mind what your intentions were. You never knew how umpires were going to react. They might call a play one way and then five seconds later call the same thing differently. You never knew. Why tempt them?

Anderson knew a lot of kids who did not listen. He wondered if the runner had ever been told such a thing or if she simply didn't remember. Either way, neither he nor Sofia would have trotted back in fair territory.

The next batter struck out in four pitches. The parents yelled, *Good cut. Get 'em next time.*

Anderson did not think the swing was a good cut at all. The batter turned her head down the third base line with every swing. With her eyes out of position, how was she supposed to hit the ball?

Players swung at pitches that were out of the strike zone. They bobbled ground balls. A runner on second could have advanced on a grounder hit to the right side of the infield but chose not to run. The thought dawned on Anderson that these players did not really know how to play.

He and Sofia had been taught how to play. They knew every nuance. They had been hauled to practice after practice. They had been hauled to camp after camp. They had been hauled to batting cage after batting cage. Even when they weren't being hauled physically, they were being hauled verbally. Mom and Dad would impart knowledge about how to round first base. Mom and Dad taught them how to charge ground balls. Mom and Dad even taught them to run with their batting gloves wadded up in their hands to prevent jamming a finger when sliding.

So much of their lives centered around playing ball that Anderson could not even fathom not knowing how to play.

Anderson took a look over at the ketchup. He was going to dedicate this baseball season to Sofia.

CHAPTER SIX

They all went to the bathroom. Well, they all
went *into* the bathroom. Mom had plugged in the
hair trimmer and put towels down on the floor. They
brought a chair from the kitchen and put it in front of
the mirror.

Dad sat down first. He squeezed Sofia's hand, and
Mom turned on the trimmer. She started taking hair
off the top of Dad's head. Mom carved out the middle,
but Dad still had tufts on the sides.

Mom said, "How about we leave it like this?"

Dad opened his eyes as wide as he could and made
a crazy-looking face.

Sofia laughed.

Dad reached up with his hand bent into the shape of a claw. He reached over for Sofia, but she retreated to the corner. She said, "It's not claw time."

"It's claw time." He reached over for her, and she laughed.

Mom finished shaving Dad's head. Anderson thought Dad looked legit — like some sort of weird professional wrestler.

Dad brushed off some strands and stood up. He looked in the mirror. "I like this," he said.

Anderson sat down. Mom buzzed the hair off the sides of his head. "You have a mullet now, Anderson."

Sofia said, "Leave it. Do it."

"No," Anderson said. "Please. I beg you."

Mom kept shaving. Hair fell to the floor. The paleness of Anderson's scalp . . . Geez, he looked like a cave monster, but he stood up, brushed away the remains, and said he liked it.

Sofia shaved Mom into, well, Mom ended up looking like some sort of shaved cat. They took a selfie, and Mom posted that they had shaved their heads to support Sofia.

Anderson hustled onto the baseball field. As usual, no other players had arrived.

Coach sat in the dugout. He said, "Anderson, nice shave-job."

"I look like a cave monster."

"It's for a great cause."

Anderson took his bat, grabbed a ball, and went to the fence. He tossed the ball up and hit it into the fence. He grabbed the ball, tossed it up again, and smacked it into the fence. Other players came lollygagging from the parking lot.

Coach yelled, "This ain't the Bigs, you know. We hustle here."

Once practice actually started, the players hustled.

Anderson put on a batting helmet and hustled to first base. He wadded up his batting gloves in his fists so he wouldn't jam a finger if he had to slide. He told himself the trip around the bases was for Sofia.

Coach said, "Anderson's going first to third. Let's make a play on him." Coach hit a ball into the gap in right-center.

Anderson got up on his toes and sprinted. He rounded second. The outfielder fielded and threw, but his momentum was going out towards center. Anderson slid. His foot hit the bag. The ball bounced into the third baseman's glove. Safe.

Coach said, "Nice hustle, Anders! That's what it takes! If we want to win state, that's what it takes! If we want to win regionals, that's what it takes! If we want to win the Little League World Series, that's what it takes! Now, men, let's start kicking some butt and having some fun!"

When the announcer called Anderson's name, Anderson hustled out to the pitcher's mound. The guys took off their hats for the Star Spangled Banner, and as the song played, Anderson got pumped. He was ready. This was the state tournament. This game was for Sofia.

The umpire yelled, *Play ball!*

Coach wanted a fastball, and so did Anderson.

The pitch . . . The batter was taking all the way.

The ball popped the leather of Charlie's mitt. The umpire yelled, *Steeee-riiiiiiike one!*

Tater Tot began chattering. *Way to fire, Anders! Way to fire!*

Coach called for a fastball. Anderson agreed. More heat. He leaned back and delivered a missile right down the middle. The batter swung and missed.

The umpire yelled, *Steeee-riiiiiiike two!*

All of the infielders got excited. They pounded their fists into their gloves and chattered.

Anderson's teammates urged him to sit the batter down, to throw strikes, to attack the zone, to bring it. Anderson wanted to keep bringing it.

Coach gave the sign, a heater.

The showdown, the pitch . . . *Steeee-riiiiiiike three! Batter out.*

The heat worked. Anderson scorched batter after batter until the fourth. He stepped off the mound to wipe the sweat out of his eyes. He saw Mom and Dad arriving late with Sofia. They set up some collapsible chairs near the fence. They never sat near the fence, but Sofia had been losing her balance more often. She probably didn't want to sit in the bleachers.

The words Anderson hated came and buzzed around his head. Anderson took a deep breath. He got the signal, an off-speed curve. Coach wanted Anderson to switch speeds and set up the batter for a strikeout. Anderson delivered. The batter lined a shot between shortstop and third base.

The words Anderson hated might as well have been mosquitoes. They flew in his eyes and landed on the back of his ears and neck. Anderson could not swat the pests away. They ate at him and stung him.

Coach called for a fastball. Anderson felt like throwing the ball past the batter, through Charlie's mitt, through the umpire, and through the backstop.

This batter was going down. Anderson felt certain the batter was guessing fastball, but he didn't care.

Anderson gritted his teeth. He stepped back into the wind-up, raised his leg, and fired.

The batter swung late.

The umpire yelled, *Steeee-riiiiiiike one!*

The words Anderson hated buzzed louder. Coach wanted a slider, low and inside. Anderson shook him off. Coach signaled for a fastball. Anderson accepted. He wanted to battle. He wanted to throw heat until his arm fell off. He wound up and gunned another missile down the middle of the plate.

The batter swung and missed. *Steeee-riiiiiike two!*

Coach didn't even give a signal. He just nodded his head. Anderson knew Coach wanted a fastball, and Anderson was happy to oblige.

The pitch . . . *Struck him out!*

Charlie tossed the ball back to the mound. The defense hustled back to the dugout.

The words Anderson hated grew silent. The heat burned them away. Anderson rode his scorcher to victory, a two-hit shutout.

After the game, he went over to Sofia. She was busy eating a hotdog that was doused in ketchup, but she took one hand off the bun and gave Anderson a fist bump.

CHAPTER SEVEN

In game one of the regional tournament, Anderson came up to the plate. It was the top of the first with runners on second and third, just one out. He was jacked out of his mind with determination.

Anderson dug in. He eyed the ball while it was in the pitcher's hand and as it approached the plate. It looked as big as a basketball, but Anderson swung and missed. He stepped out of the box.

Tater Tot stood on second base. His chatter came in loud and clear. *Drive us in, Anders. Let's go, buddy.*

Anderson wanted to thank Tator Tot for the wonderful advice.

Instead, he concentrated on the sign. Coach signaled for Anderson to swing away, as if Anderson had any doubts.

The pitcher wound up. He threw. A fat curve looped low toward the plate. Anderson tried to golf it but fouled off a dribbler for strike two.

Tater ran his mouth. *Drive us in, Anders. Let's go, now, buddy.*

Coach's sign: Swing away.

Anderson took a practice swing and stepped into the box. The pitch . . . Anderson stepped and swung.

As the bat smashed into the ball, Anderson could tell he made solid contact. The feel and the noise, oh man. He lined a bomb to deep left.

Back, back, back, back, back. *Gone!*

A three-run shot in the top of the first. Anderson hustled around the bases as fast as he could. He sped around third and saw Sofia sitting near the fence in her collapsible chair. He pumped his fist at her.

Sofia held up her ketchup-doused hotdog in salute. Anderson and crew won in a route.

In game two of regionals, with a score of 0-0 in the bottom of the fourth inning, the opponent got runners on first and third with two outs. The batter hit a pop-foul to shallow left. Anderson charged from shortstop into foul territory. He had a chance.

He put his hand on the fence to position himself. He jumped and leaned over. Anderson caught the ball but lost his balance. He fell over the fence. Some spectators tried to cushion his fall. Anderson hit the ground hard, but he held on to the ball and killed the other team's rally.

He tossed the ball to Sofia. She sat by the fence in her collapsible chair. She had on a cap and sunglasses.

"Oh, thanks a lot," Sofia said as she caught the ball. She threw it back onto the field, and Anderson laughed as he ran back to shortstop.

In the top of the fifth, Charlie hit a two-run homer that was the difference maker.

In the next game of regionals, a dogfight ensued.

Anderson and company trailed by five runs after the top half of the first. They countered by scoring two in the bottom of the inning and added one more on an Anderson home run in the bottom of the third. In the bottom of the fourth, Tater drove in two runs with a liner to right but was called out sliding into second.

The game was tied 5–5 going into the sixth.

Anderson readied himself at shortstop. The batter chopped one in between short and third. The ball bounced so high in the air that Anderson had no play by the time he fielded the ball.

Tater, who was playing second base, got his chatter going. *Let's turn two, Anders. Let's turn two!*

Anderson held two fingers in the air as if to say, *Yes, let's turn two and get a double play.*

The batter worked the count full. Then, a lazy ground ball came bouncing to Tater's right. Tater barehanded the ball. His momentum carried him away from the bag, so he flipped the ball to Anderson, who hustled over to cover second. Anderson caught the toss from Tater, dragged his foot over second base, and machine-gunned the ball to first.

The umpire was not as vocal as others in the profession. Blue made a fist and stuck up his thumb. The runner was out. Double play.

Coach jumped off the bench and clapped. "Nice hustle! Tater, great play! Anders, way to fire!"

The next batter hit a dribbler to first. The first baseman snagged the ball and stepped on the bag.

Anderson led off the bottom of the sixth. Coach ran through a series of meaningless signals, all of which meant the same thing, to swing away. Anderson stood with one foot in the batter's box. He tamped the dirt and took a practice swing.

He looked over and saw Sofia staring at him. She held up her fist, daring him to start a rally.

Anderson got all jacked up with determination. He eyed the ball in the pitcher's hand and zeroed in as the ball approached. He tried to hit the ball with his hands. The bat followed Anderson's hands and made contact with the ball, driving it to the right-center gap.

Coach yelled, "Get on your horse!"

Anderson got up on his toes and sprinted. The right fielder and center fielder tried to catch up with the ball. Anderson rounded first and dug in for second. The ball bounced off the fence and rolled back to the right fielder. Anderson rounded second and looked to Third Base Coach for the signal. The signal was *Go to third!*

From the dugout, Coach yelled, "Go three, Anderson! Go three!"

Anderson dug down and shifted into the highest gear he had.

The right fielder fired the ball to the second baseman. The second baseman caught the ball, spun, and gunned it to third. The throw came in to third base at shoulder level. The third baseman caught the ball. Anderson slid. The third baseman applied the tag. The umpire held out his arms as if they were a pair of wings. *Safe.*

Coach was all fired up. "Nice hustle, Anders! That's what it takes! Get up! Dust yourself off and have some fun!"

Third Base Coach patted Anderson on the back. Anderson saw Sofia struggle to her feet. She steadied herself and clapped with all the energy she had.

Anderson brushed off his uniform. He wadded up his batting gloves and held them in his fists. He checked the signals. They had a runner on third with no outs. Obviously: *Swing away.*

The batter swung at the first pitch. A bloop to center fell in, and Anderson scored the winning run.

Coaches and teammates did not mob each other at the plate. They had won the game, but that's what they were supposed to do. Besides, they still had to win one more game to qualify for the Little League World Series.

The winning team shook hands with the losing team, and they all wished each other the best.

As Anderson gathered his things, he saw Sofia lose balance. Mom and Dad wrapped their arms around her. They helped her keep her footing.

Anderson grabbed a bat and sat down on the dugout's bench. He had thought Sofia was going to have a good day. She had been eating hotdogs. She had thrown the ball back onto the field. But now, she was losing her balance again. Anderson twisted the end of the bat into the dugout floor with as much strength as he could muster.

CHAPTER EIGHT

The next day, before the regional championship game, Anderson warmed up in the bullpen. He could feel his scorcher coming alive.

Coach said to come on in. It was game time. He said, "I don't need to tell you, but I'm going to tell you. If we win, we're in. We're in the Little League World Series. This is why we've hustled. This is why we've brushed dirt off our pants. This is why we've had so much fun."

Some players pounded their fists into their mitts.

Coach said, "Do you know what we're going to do?"

Some players said, "Hustle!"

"No," Coach said. "We're going to have fun. On the count of three. One. Two. Three."

Everyone yelled, *Have fun!*

The players took their positions.

Anderson toed the rubber and received the sign for a fastball. He wound up. The ball might as well have been shot out of a cannon. The batter flailed at the pitch, and somehow made contact, a pop-up behind the plate. Charlie sprung to his feet, threw off his mask, spotted the ball, turned around, and made the catch. He threw it around the horn.

Coach called for more heat. The batter? Forget it. He whiffed in four pitches, all fastballs. He was lucky to foul tip one at all.

More heat. The batter swung and missed. The ball snapped the leather of Charlie's mitt.

Tater Tot chattered. *Way to fire, Anders. Way to fire. C'mon now, buddy.*

Two more fastballs, two more strikes. After one inning, Anderson had yet to throw a ball.

The team put three runs on the board in the bottom of the first. Anderson came back to the mound. He had determination clamped upon his face. He was ready to throw some heat. The warm-ups were all strikes. His wind-up felt great. Coach went through a series of signals even though everyone from the batter to the people watching from the stands knew Anderson was going to throw a fastball.

Anderson wound up and fired. The batter did not swing, not that he could have hit the pitch regardless, but the ball came in an inch high.

Anderson fired, and again the batter did not swing. This time the ball was right down the middle. The umpire called out, *Steeee-riiiiiiike!*

Anderson threw a slider that appeared to cross the outside edge of the plate, but the batter did not swing. The umpire called the pitch a ball.

The thought occurred to Anderson that perhaps this batter was not going to swing at anything. Since the batter could not touch Anderson's heat, the plan was to stand there and hope for a walk — this was their cleanup hitter, no less. Anderson did not like that kind of attitude.

Anderson reared back and launched a fastball down the middle. The batter did not swing. *Steeee-riiiiiiike two!*

The count was two and two. Both Anderson and Coach suspected the batter was not going to swing, so the call was for another fastball. Anderson delivered.

The batter did not swing. The pitch buzzed the outside corner of the plate, but the ump called a ball.

With two strikes, the batter should have been protecting. Obviously, this dude was up there looking for a walk. Anderson threw another fastball that appeared to hit the outside corner, but the ump called another ball. The batter took first.

The next guy hit a drubber in front of home plate. The ball stopped right in the middle of Anderson and Charlie, and neither of them had a play. Now, because of dubious umpiring and a fluke hit, the opponent had runners on first and second with no outs.

Batter number six came up and took some powerful practice swings. Anderson threw a fastball with as much strength as he could muster. The noise of the bat hitting the ball sounded dangerous. A line drive headed deep to left. The left fielder sprinted back but could not make a play. It was a home run.

As the batter rounded the bases, Anderson could feel himself coming unraveled, but he had made a vow, a dedication, to play the rest of the season for Sofia.

Sofia sat by the fence. She gave him a thumbs-up. The score was even. He might as well reset and get back to work.

Steeee-riiiiiiike! called the ump.

Steeee-riiiiiiike two!

Steeee-riiiiiiike three, batter out!

Forget it. No one got another hit off Anderson the rest of the afternoon. Tater Tot drove in a run in the fifth to decide the game.

After shaking hands with the other team, Anderson and company did some fist-bumping but did not get too excited. Sure, they were going to the Little League World Series, but they were not yet ready to celebrate.

Some doctors wanted Sofia to come stay at a treatment center right away. Other doctors thought a treatment center was not yet necessary. Everyone did agree, however, that Sofia's condition had gotten worse. Moving her to a treatment center was a matter of when, not if.

She was sick all the time, but today Sofia was the guest of honor at her softball team's game. She sat in the dugout in her uniform. She wore a blue bandana.

The bandana's color matched the blue ribbons sewn on the girls' uniforms. When the players and coaches returned from taking infield, Sofia said to her coach, "I can't throw the first pitch."

Her coach said, "Okay."

Sofia stood up and steadied herself. "I can't sit in here, either."

The coach helped her exit the dugout. All the girls gave her a fist bump as she walked by.

Sofia joined Anderson, Mom, and Dad and sat in a collapsible chair along the fence. Anderson asked Sofia if she wanted a hotdog, but she said she didn't want one. Anderson did want one but decided he shouldn't.

The announcer called the players' names and positions. Mr. Announcer then turned people's attention to Sofia. She stood and shook her head. She didn't want the attention. Mom and Dad got up to help her keep her balance.

Mr. Announcer said Sofia hit .410 last season while winning eighteen games as a pitcher. Fans discovered Sofia had a .998 fielding percentage while playing first base. People stood and clapped their hands. When Mr. Announcer mentioned the ribbons on the girls' uniforms were in honor of Sofia, the crowd went nuts, cheering and whistling.

Sofia's face turned red. She rolled her eyes and swallowed. Mom tried to hug her, but Sofia did not want to be hugged. She turned to Anderson and said, "Can I get a hotdog?"

"Let's go," said Anderson.

The applause died down.

Anderson helped Sofia walk to the concession stand, and of course, the lady selling hotdogs wanted Sofia to have one for free. Sofia accepted but made Anderson put two bucks in the tip jar.

Sofia's team? Well, execution of routine plays was a problem.

In the first inning, the pitcher got her glove on a ball hit up the middle, but she did not field it cleanly. The ball bounded off her glove toward the girl playing third, and the girl playing third had no play.

Anderson noticed Sofia was not eating her hotdog. He didn't know if it was because her team was playing so poorly or if it was because she had no appetite. Maybe some of both.

A batter lined one to left. The left fielder dove for the ball and almost made the catch but didn't. The center fielder tracked down the ball but not before a run scored.

The catcher could have caught a pop foul but got too twisted around to make the play.

Sofia said to Anderson, "Can I play on your team?"

"As long as you don't chatter."

"Not at all?" she said.

"No," said Anderson. "Tater Tot chatters enough for everyone."

Mom chimed in. "Sofia was the glue. Without her, these girls are unfocused."

Anderson said, "You're the glue, Sofia. You're like a bottle of Elmer's."

Sofia said, "Shut your piehole, Anders."

CHAPTER NINE

A week later, Anderson woke up thinking about waffles smothered in peanut butter and about two or three glasses of milk to wash it all down. Maybe he could talk Mom into frying some bacon. He could put the bacon on the waffles and then completely suffocate them in peanut butter. *Oh man,* he thought. *Where's Mom?*

She wasn't in the kitchen. He looked outside. She wasn't outside. No one was in the living room. She was probably in Sofia's room. Now that Sofia had moved into the treatment center, Mom liked to sit in Sofia's room and drink a cup of coffee.

The door to Sofia's room was cracked open. Anderson could see Mom sitting on Sofia's bed and sipping coffee.

Anderson pushed open the door. He said, "Mom, you thinking bacon? What say we fry up some pork?"

Mom had red around her eyes. She put her coffee cup on the floor and held out her arms for Anderson to come give her a hug. Anderson wrapped his arms around her.

Mom rested her cheek on the side of Anderson's neck. Anderson could feel the heat of her tears. "She's going to pull through," Mom said. "I know it."

Acute. Lymphoblastic. Leukemia. Anemia. Radiation. Port. Chemotherapy. Hemorrhage. Pulmonary system. Infection. Anderson hated these words more than ever.

He started hating Sofia's doctors. They were the ones who had given him all the words he hated. They explained so many possibilities . . .

Anderson couldn't understand. He was sick of them sending tissue samples to the lab. He was sick of waiting. He was sick of everything. If they couldn't make Sofia get well, he was going to punch them.

At the treatment center, Sofia lay in bed asleep. She had tubes attached to her nose and arms.

Anderson started punching his chair.

The outline of Sofia's port was visible under the blankets. Her chest hardly moved up and down when she breathed.

Anderson stood up and started punching the air.

Dad escorted Anderson outside.

Outside, Anderson threw himself down and started punching the grass. Dad let him go. To Dad, Anderson looked like a kid who just needed to be left alone.

Aunt Jo, Uncle Brad, Cousin Nate, and Cousin Clay came to visit. They would help sat the house while Mom and Dad stayed with Sofia at the treatment center.

Cousin Nate and Cousin Clay wanted to play baseball. They got Anderson out to the yard, but Anderson missed good pitches and intentionally missed balls hit right to him. He didn't care. Aunt Jo saw what he was doing and made him come inside. She tried to comfort him but couldn't find the right words. She let him go to his room and play games on his phone. The games he played reminded him of Sofia: *Minecraft*, and especially *Ogre's Ice Cream*. He put his face in his pillow and stayed like that until it became hard to breathe.

Anderson could hardly think about baseball. Uncle Brad took him and Nate and Clay to the ball diamond for some batting practice. Nate and Clay said they wanted to pitch. They said if Anderson was going to play in the Little League World Series, then he would need to face pitchers as good as they were. Anderson didn't laugh. He knew they were joking, but he was not in the mood.

Anderson blooped a few into shallow right. He blooped a few into shallow left.

Uncle Brad told Nate to come in and hit. Anderson retreated to the bench. He watched his relatives attempt to have fun. Nate hit a grounder to first base. Clay kind of tried to field the ball but not really.

Anderson thought of Sofia. Sofia played first base when she was not pitching. She never would have let a grounder like that get the best of her. Then again, Sofia never would have stood at the plate like Anderson had done and blooped a few into the outfield. Sofia would have driven the ball.

Anderson started thinking about his vow, his dedication, his declaration that the rest of his season was for Sofia. Was it all for nothing?

Mom and Dad came home to spend some time with Anderson. They sat him down at the computer and bought plane tickets to Williamsport, Pennsylvania, home of the Little League World Series.

Dad said, "Anders, my man, Sofia wants you to keep playing hard."

Anderson agreed. Sofia would definitely want him to keep playing hard.

After they purchased tickets, Anderson headed out to the garage, got on his bike, and went to the ball field. He did not turn on the lights. He sat with his back against the backstop and looked out at the diamond. The words Anderson hated swarmed like angry insects inside his head. Real insects started biting him, but Anderson didn't even care. He sat there, with his bites swelling, and stared out at the bases.

In Williamsport, Coach chose Anderson to be the starting pitcher. Anderson's defense helped as much as they could, but they could only get their gloves on hard hit balls for two innings. In the third, line drives were hit all over the place.

Anderson gave up five runs. His team could not counter. In the fourth, Anderson gave up another two. Before the inning ended, Coach came out. Coach patted Anderson on the back. He said, "Anders, go ahead and take a seat."

The Little League World Series is a double elimination tournament. They would have another chance, but Anderson was mad anyway. In the dugout, he took his bat and rubbed it as hard as he could into the dugout floor.

After the game, Mom wanted to go out to eat. She and Dad were both worried about Sofia. Aunt Jo and Uncle Brad were taking shifts at the treatment center, but Mom still hated to be away. Mom chose a Mexican restaurant because of Sofia's fondness for enchiladas. Anderson thought hotdogs doused in ketchup would be a better tribute, but he didn't say it.

Mom pulled some Uno cards out of a handbag. Mom dealt. Dad and Mom let Anderson win until he realized what was happening. Then, Anderson caught fire. He played some wild cards. He made his parents draw four. He reversed the order. Mom and Dad called "Uno," but the calling made no difference. Anderson was going to make them draw four. If Sofia were here, she would have really piled it on.

They paid the bill and went back to the hotel.

Sleep?

They went deep into the count against sleep. Their uneasiness about Sofia fouled off some balls. Anderson grabbed an extra pillow and protected the plate. He held the pillow up to his face, so Mom and Dad couldn't hear him crying. And upon further review, the umpire called Anderson safe.

CHAPTER TEN

Anderson sat in a chair in the shower of the hotel. Mom turned on the hair trimmer. The blades hummed and vibrated back and forth. She gave Anderson a fresh buzz.

Dad came in. He said, "You know, I like this buzzed look. I might keep it."

Mom said Dad looked like a madman.

Dad said, "Yeah, that's the point." Dad made his hand into a claw. He tormented Anderson with it.

Anderson did not find the routine funny at all but laughed anyway. He tried to stop and found that he couldn't.

Dad kept his stupid claw-hand in Anderson's face. Hair fell down. The trimmer buzzed. Dad groaned like a monster. Anderson laughed and laughed and laughed.

Coach marched back and forth in the dugout. "Coming back after a loss," he said, "is the most important thing you can do in life. Forget baseball. I'm talking about life!"

Anderson wondered if the speech was aimed at him.

Coach went on. "If you stay down after a loss, you might stay down forever. You have to get up. I'm talking about living. I'm talking about fighting. I'm talking about swinging for the fence in life. I'm talking about sliding headfirst. I'm talking about beating out throws, throws that might kill you, the junk life throws at you, the fastballs at head-level, the bad calls — you'd better run! You'd better hustle.

You'd better take some cracks. If you get cheated, it's your own fault. If you can't get around the bases, it's your own fault. If you can't even compete, it's your own fault. Now let's get out there and have some fun!"

They got around the bases. Twelve times. They hustled so hard that the other team looked like it was moving in slow motion.

They didn't slow down in the next game. In fact, they sped up. They put fourteen on the board.

Anderson gave up one run in three innings. He amassed eight strikeouts and was pulled because Coach didn't want him going over the league's pitch count.

Run production blasted into space. They scored twenty the next game. The other team couldn't wait to leave.

Anderson threw two scoreless innings in the next game and took four strikeouts to the bank.

The offense slugged its way to ten runs. If the energy from their hustle and the force of their swings could have been harnessed, the team could have taken flight.

For the championship game, Coach said, "We aren't done. We aren't done bouncing back. The bounce is not complete. Our lives are still in danger. If we stumble, we might go down. We might not get up again, ever, in life. We must swing for the fence and run for our lives. Now let's get out there and have some fun!"

Anderson took the mound. His arm felt ready to fire. His mind felt ready to light it up.

The pitch . . . Fastball in for a strike.

On the next pitch, the batter grounded to Tater Tot. Tater threw him out. One down.

The next man flew out to the left, and the hitter in the three-spot grounded to first. Anderson got through the inning throwing only five pitches.

Another onslaught of runs came in the bottom of the first. Anderson doubled to drive in Tater Tot. The team put up four in the first.

Second inning. Anderson got the signal. Coach wanted a fastball. A fastball he was going to get. Anderson wound up and fired. The batter swung and missed.

Chatter flooded from Tater Tot. *Way to fire, Anders. Way to go.*

Coach wanted a set-up pitch, a hard slider inside. Charlie set the target, and Anderson located the pitch perfectly. The batter watched it bend into the strike zone. Now a fastball outside ought to sit him down.

The pitch . . . *Strike three!*

Way to fire, Anders. Way to Fire!

The next batter hammered a shot foul down the left field line. If the ball had fallen two inches to the right, the batter would have had at least a double. Anderson thought about his vow, his dedication.

He would still have to do better. The bounce was not complete.

Anderson threw an off-speed curve. The batter was way out in front for strike two. Now Anderson wanted a fastball down the middle. He wanted to battle. He didn't care if the batter knew what was coming. He wanted to see if the batter could hit some heat. Coach called for heat. Charlie set the target. Anderson wound up and reared back. The batter swung and missed and walked like a jerk back to the dugout.

Anderson threw his first ball to the next hitter. Then, Anderson missed high with a fastball and went down 2-0. The batter was late on the next pitch but fouled it hard down the right field line. Anderson missed low on the next pitch, and for some reason, he started thinking about the game he and Sofia had played, the one at the ballpark, the one in which Anderson had to strike her out three times before he could hit.

Anderson wanted a fastball. He wanted to battle. Anderson scorched a heater down the middle. The batter swung and missed.

The count was 3-2. Coach wanted a curveball, which sounded good to Anderson. The pitch . . . Foul tip.

All right, a follow-up fastball should do it. Anderson wound up. He gritted his teeth.

The batter swung and missed for strike three to end the inning. Anderson could imagine Sofia rolling her eyes affectionately.

The runs came in droves. It was almost as if they were playing an easy video game. A series of singles, followed by a double and a home run allowed another four runs. They were up 8-0 going into the third.

Anderson's resolve remained strong. He got three outs on only six pitches, and the other team's coach started yelling about working the counts and making the pitcher work.

Anderson thought they could work the counts as much as they wanted. He would battle regardless, and he would emerge victorious.

The offense erupted, even by their standards, scoring seven more runs to go up 15-0 going into the fourth.

The opponents jogged back to the dugout with their heads down. Their coach tried to fire them up. He said, "Hey, we aren't done."

Coach stopped the defense on their way out to the field. Coach said, "We aren't done either. The bounce is not yet complete. Now, hustle!"

Anderson got so focused he wasn't even aware he was focused. He fired without thinking and felt like he was a step ahead of everyone else in the game. He was possibly a step ahead of everyone else in the world.

He played catch with Charlie and thought about funny things Sofia liked to do. She doused her stupid hotdogs in so much ketchup that the bun looked like it was soaked in blood. Anderson could practically see her in the stands munching away. And then, of course, her attitude was relentless when she played Uno. What in the world was that? You would have thought the game was a matter of life and death. She played all of those wild cards, reverses, and draw fours. Girl, chill out. Seriously?

When Anderson came back to the real world, he had two outs in the top of the sixth. They were one out away from winning the Little League World Series. The weight of everything finally crept up. Anderson bounced one in the dirt.

The other team's coach took off his hat and said, "He finally missed. It's a miracle."

Tater Tot chattered. *Let's go, Anders. Let's fire. Complete the bounce, buddy. Complete the bounce.*

Anderson got a big lump in his throat. He swallowed. He wound up and launched a missile. *Strike one.*

All of the players, all of the spectators, all of the people watching at home could tell which team was going to win. But Anderson was one out away from throwing a no-hitter in the championship game of the Little League World Series. He would be featured on TV later. Anderson stepped off the mound. He took off his cap and ran his hand over his shaved head.

Suddenly, he felt terrified, but he could see Sofia rolling her eyes. He remembered his vow.

Coach called for a fastball, but Anderson shook him off. Anderson was in the mood for a slow curve. It would be like Sofia playing a wild card.

Anderson wound up and delivered. The batter swung and hit a slow roller back to the mound. Anderson fielded the ball. He took a few steps toward first and tossed the ball on over.

The first baseman caught the ball. The umpire called the batter out. Coach ran out of the dugout. "The bounce! It's over! We did it! It's done!"

Anderson threw his arms up. The infielders hugged. The outfielders ran as fast as they could into the infield, where the team would finally celebrate. The back-up players ran out of the dugout. Charlie grabbed Anderson and picked him up.

The lump in Anderson's throat returned. Tears ran down his cheeks. His chest started heaving. He didn't care. He had dedicated the season to Sofia and had emerged a champion. The victory was for both of them.

The team mobbed him. They joined in with Charlie and held him up. *A no-hitter in the championship game of the Little League World Series?* Anderson raised his arms to the sky. He let tears roll down his cheeks. The cameras came onto the field. The reporters lined up.

Mom and Dad made their way through the throngs. They were both sobbing. The players put Anderson down, and Mom and Dad hugged him as tightly as they could.

Dad said, "She's proud of you, Anders! She's proud! We're proud!"

Mom showed Anderson a picture Sofia had texted. Sofia was sitting up in bed holding a piece of paper that said, *Seriously? A no-hitter? Congratulations!*

The other team came out and gave their regards. Their coach told Anderson, "I've never seen anything like that. You guys deserve it. You're a warrior."

Anderson could not respond. His chest heaved. Tears ran down his face. His eyes were hardly open. All he knew was that when things calmed down, he was going to go to the concession stand. He was going to get a hotdog. He was going to douse that thing in ketchup, and he was going to savor every last bite.

AUTHOR BIO

Derek Tellier, as a child, dreamed big. He played baseball, hustled, and made very few errors. After going deep in the count and fouling off pitch after pitch, he earned a Master of Fine Arts degree in Creative Writing from Minnesota State University, Mankato. His writing has appeared in *Secret Laboratory, New Verse News,* and *Ascent Aspirations.* He is a writer, musician, and teacher in the Twin Cities.

GLOSSARY

all-stars—the best players from every team in a league

barehanded—fielding a ball without using a glove, usually to save time and make a quick throw

bunt—when the batter waives the bat to make light contact and push the ball out in front of home plate or down a baseline

chopper—a ground ball, usually hard hit, that bounces numerous times before reaching a fielder

double—when the batter hits the ball so hard that he or she can run from home plate to second base

line drive—a fly ball that is hit very hard

pop up—a ball hit lightly but very high in the air

shortstop—infield position between second and third base

triple—when the batter hits the ball so hard that he or she can run from home plate to third base

DISCUSSION QUESTIONS

I. *Anderson's Heat* is the title of this story. What does the title mean to you? Could it have more than one meaning?

2. One of Anderson's teammates is nicknamed Tator Tot. Do you have a nickname? How did you get it?

3. The story of Anderson's team making it to the Little League World Series takes on greater meaning after Sofia gets cancer. Have you ever had a situation get more serious as it goes on?

WRITING PROMPTS

1. Anderson and Sofia have a key to the baseball diamond. Have you ever been trusted with property that other kids could not be trusted with? Has a grown-up ever trusted you to do something that required a lot of responsibility? Tell a story about getting the key to something special.

2. Anderson has a high baseball IQ. He knows a lot about baseball. What's something you know a lot about? Is it a game? Some sort of competition? Is it cooking macaroni and cheese? Write an essay on this thing you know a lot about and share it with someone who might not know.

3. Sofia likes hotdogs. She loves them. What food do you love? What makes it so good?